This **Walker** book
belongs to:

_____

_____

_____

A Note to Grown-ups

Isn't happiness an amazing feeling! It makes me want to sing and dance,
just like this puppy. When you read this book with a young child, you can explore
their own feelings: what makes you both happy? Things you like eating?
Places you like to go? People you like to see? Playing, reading books, watching TV?
You can even come up with crazy fantasy things that would make you happy
and think what being happy feels like, just like this puppy.
Help children explore their imagination – a place
where anything can happen!

For Joni, love Zeyde Mick. M.R.

For Elsie and Elliot, and all the joy they bring us. R.S.

First published 2023 by Walker Books Ltd, 87 Vauxhall Walk, London SE11 5HJ

This edition published 2023

2 4 6 8 10 9 7 5 3 1

Text © 2023 Michael Rosen • Illustrations © 2023 Robert Starling

The right of Michael Rosen and Robert Starling to be identified as author and illustrator respectively of this work
has been asserted in accordance with the Copyright, Designs and Patents Act 1988

This work has been typeset in Futura

Printed in China

British Library Cataloguing in Publication Data: a catalogue record for this book is available from the British Library

ISBN 978-1-5295-1982-2

www.walker.co.uk

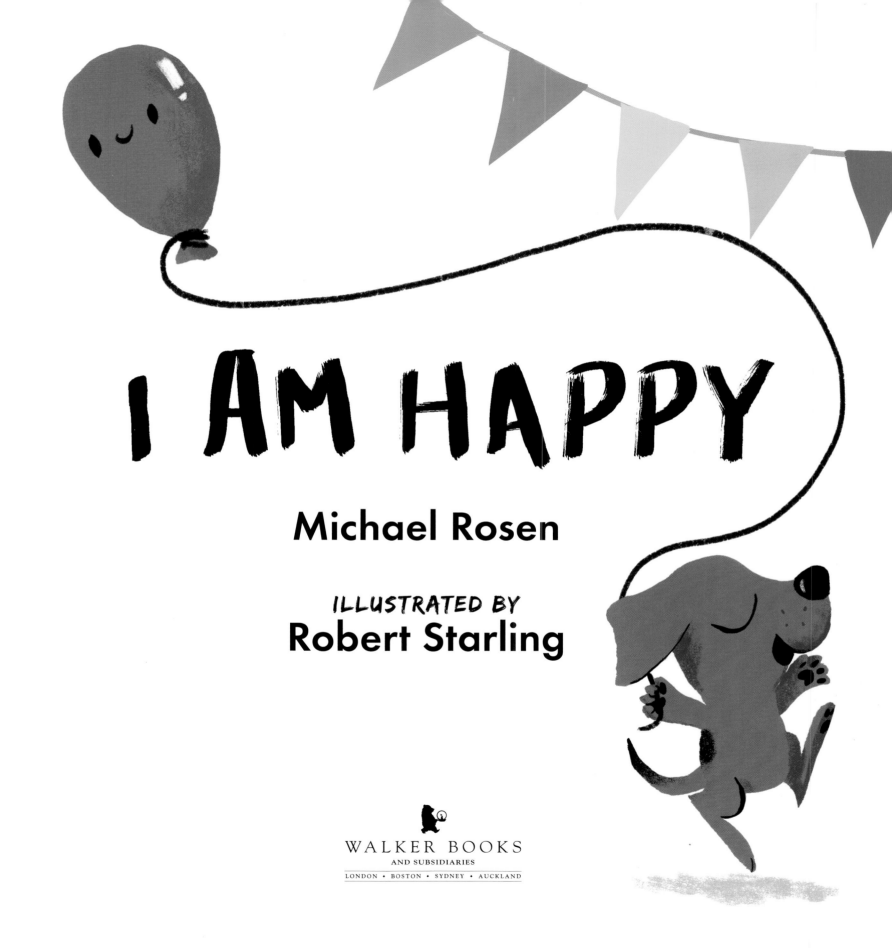

I AM HAPPY

Michael Rosen

ILLUSTRATED BY
Robert Starling

WALKER BOOKS
AND SUBSIDIARIES
LONDON • BOSTON • SYDNEY • AUCKLAND

I am
happy.

REALLY
happy.

Happy,

happy,

happy.

I'm SO happy I ...

sing on a swing, swing as I sing,

head in the sky,

like a butterfly.

I skip through puddles,

chase after bubbles,

dance the waltz,

do somersaults,

laugh out loud,

a cloud.

on

climb

I can walk on air,

AAK!

wind in my hair,

r-o-l-l d-o-w-n a m-o-u-n-t-a-i-n,

dance in a fountain,

zoom in cars ...

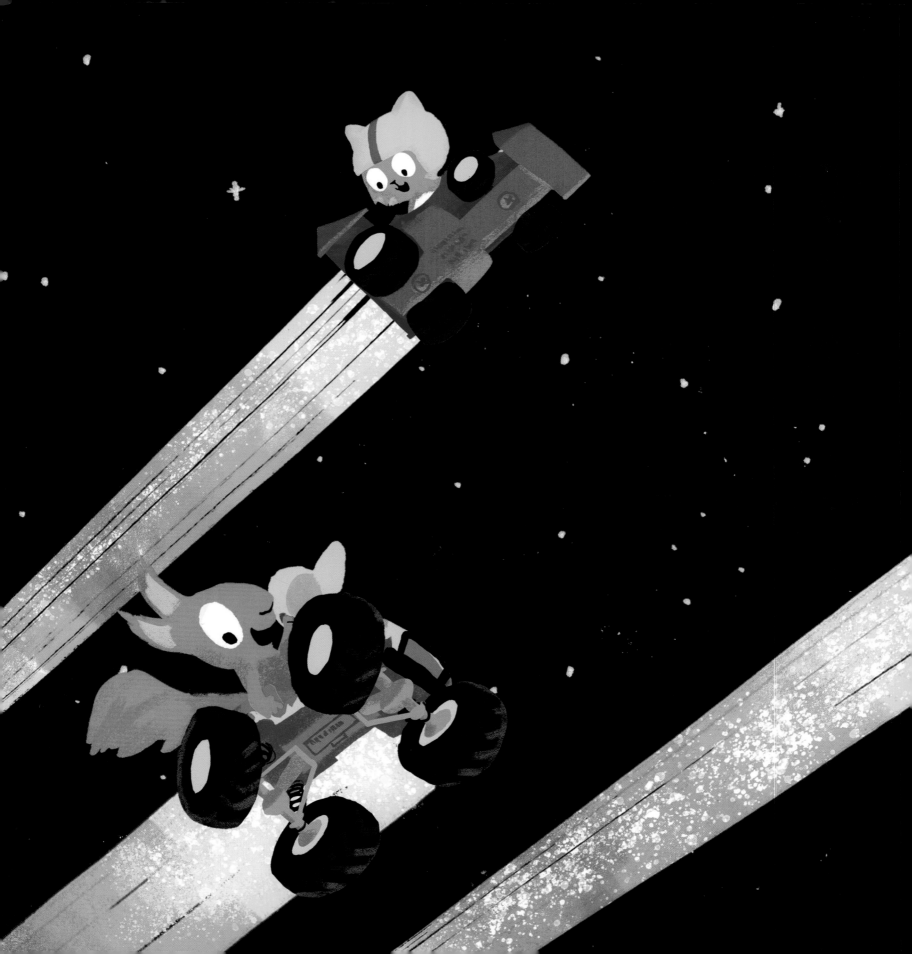

all the way to the stars.

Put on a show

hello, hello!

Wheeling and whirling,

twisting and twirling

let's play
all day!

Also in this series:

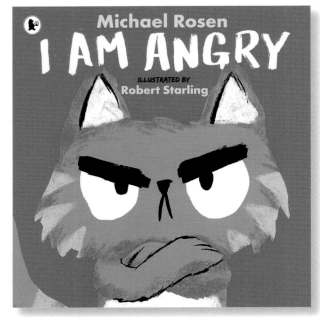

ISBN 978-1-5295-0414-9

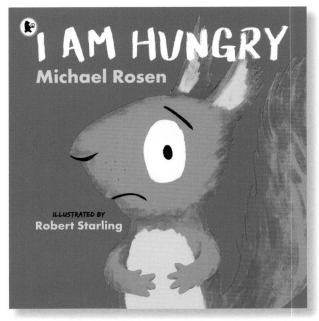

ISBN 978-1-5295-1098-0

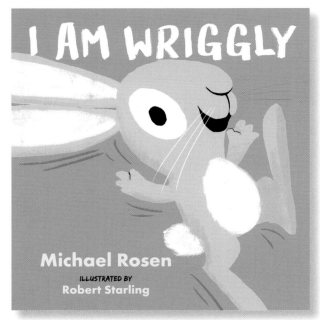

ISBN 978-1-5295-0658-7

Available from all good booksellers